For Woody – S.T.

For Konrad – K.M.

A TEMPLAR BOOK

First published in the UK in 2017 by Templar Publishing,
an imprint of Kings Road Publishing,
part of the Bonnier Publishing Group,
The Plaza, 535 King's Road, London, SW10 0SZ
www.bonnierpublishing.com

1 3 5 7 9 10 8 6 4 2

ISBN 978-1-78370-451-4

Edited by Zanna Davidson and Katie Haworth
Designed by Olivia Cook

Printed in China

I am Actually a Penguin

Written by

Sean Taylor

Illustrated by

Kasia Matyjaszek

t

templar publishing

This is **me.**

But when I put on my fancy-dress outfits,
I don't have to be me any more.

I can be a **completely**
pretty princess.

A **very**
incredible pirate.

A totally
terrible witch.

And last week, I got a new favourite outfit.

So I became an **amazingly special** . . .

. . . penguin.

I liked being a penguin **so much**,
I wore my outfit to the supermarket.

Mum asked, "Do you want
spaghetti or **lasagne?**"

I said back, "Penguins don't eat
spaghetti **or** lasagne."

Mum said, "You're not
actually a penguin!"

Frozen Foods

But that's what **she** thought.

I was **actually** a penguin all the way back home.

I was **actually** a penguin the next day.

PENGUINS

TIGERS
THIS WAY
→

And the next.

My brother had to get used to sharing the sofa with a penguin.

He asked, "Why have you put toilet paper everywhere?"

"It's **snow**," I told him. "I am **actually** a penguin,

and this is how penguins chill out."

He said, "Penguins are **dumb**."

I said, "Penguins are **COOL**."

He didn't know how to argue with that.

But he **did** like it when I stayed being a penguin for our auntie's wedding.

(One man didn't look so pleased
about my outfit. But he looked pretty
much like a penguin himself.)

My mum kept saying
I was going to **break** something.
But I still kept coming down the stairs
like a **penguin** should.

She wasn't happy when I answered the telephone and didn't actually say **anything** . . . because penguins can't talk.

And my dad tried telling me to wear pyjamas,
but he had to get used to giving a **goodnight kiss** to a penguin.

The **most** difficult moment, though, was when I got my brother to throw me fish fingers. I **thought** I could catch them in my beak.

But it was **tricky.**

Dad said,
"Listen! Everyone loves your outfit, but

YOU'RE NOT ACTUALLY A PENGUIN!"

I said back,

"I am actually a penguin."

Then Monday morning came.

That meant I had to go to school.

Mum told me, "You'll **have** to take off the outfit now."

My brother said, "You **can't** go to school dressed like that."

Dad said, "Your penguin suit needs a **wash**."

I **never** wanted to stop being a penguin.
But I went upstairs.
And I thought they **might** be right.
So I took off the penguin outfit.

And I decided I am **actually** . . .

. . . an **alligator.**

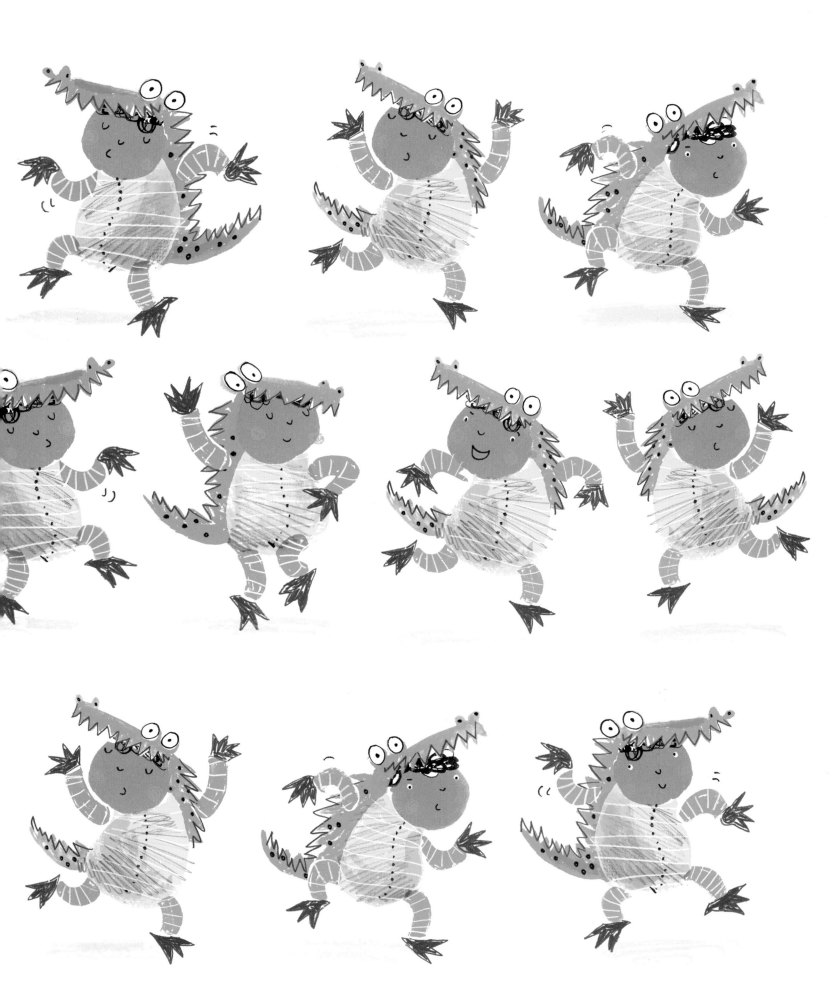

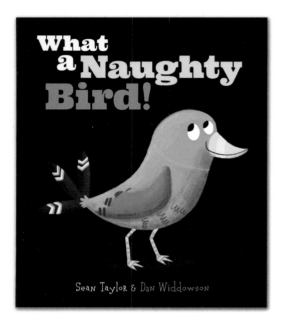

ISBN: 978-1-78370-246-6 (hardback)
978-1-78370-348-7 (paperback)

Also by Sean Taylor:
What a Naughty Bird!
A naughty bird flies around the world, pooing on other animals, until he goes too far . . . Will the naughty bird learn his lesson once and for all? A hilarious rhyming romp.

Also by Kasia Matyjaszek:
I am a very Clever Cat
Stockton is a very clever cat. He is especially clever at knitting. But is he as clever as he thinks he is, or is he going to find himself in the middle of a very knotty problem?

ISBN: 978-1-78370-591-7 (hardback)
978-1-78370-590-0 (paperback)